P9-DEB-770

GOOD DOG, ROVER

GOOD DOG, ROVER

A Bantam Book

Simultaneously published in hardcover and trade paper/September 1989
"Bantam Little Rooster" is a trademark of Bantam Books.

All rights reserved.
Text copyright © 1989 by Margo Mason.
Illustrations copyright © 1989 by Sandy Hoffman.
No part of this book may be reproduced or transmitted
in any form or by any means, electronic or mechanical,
including photocopying, recording, or by any information
storage and retrieval system, without permission in
writing from the publisher.
For information address: Bantam Books.

Library of Congress Cataloging-in-Publication Data

Mason, Margo.
  Good dog, Rover.
  "A Bantam little rooster book."
  Summary: A family adjusts to its new dog, which is really just right for them.
  [1. Dogs—Fiction] I. Hoffman, Sanford, ill.
II. Title.
PZ7.M414Gp   1989   [E]   88-8044
ISBN 0-553-05814-2
ISBN 0-553-34724-1 (pbk.)

Published simultaneously in the United States and Canada

Bantam Books are published by Bantam Books, a division of Bantam Doubleday
Dell Publishing Group, Inc. Its trademark, consisting of the words "Bantam
Books" and the portrayal of a rooster, is Registered in U.S. Patent and
Trademark Office and in other countries. Marca Registrada. Bantam Books,
666 Fifth Avenue, New York, New York 10103.

PRINTED IN THE UNITED STATES OF AMERICA

WAK   0 9 8 7 6 5 4 3 2 1

GOOD DOG, ROVER

by Margo Mason
Pictures by Sandy Hoffman

A BANTAM LITTLE ROOSTER BOOK
NEW YORK · TORONTO · LONDON · SYDNEY · AUCKLAND

My name is Andy.
My sister's name is Amy.

We are going
to adopt a dog.

Amy wants a little dog.

I want a big dog.

Mom says, "I don't like little dogs."

Dad says, "I don't like big dogs."

Amy says, "I don't like black dogs."

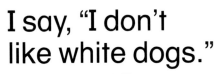

We go to the pound.
We look at lots
and lots of dogs.

Little dogs…

big dogs…

white dogs…

black dogs.

And then…

we find Rover!

Rover is not big.
He is not little.
He is not white.
He is not black.
He's just right!

Rover likes us.
We like Rover.

So we take him home.

Rover is smart.
We teach him a trick.

"Good dog!"
"Good dog!"

I teach Rover
another trick...

and another...

and another!

"Good dog, Rover!"

At dinner Rover shows us his tricks.

"No, Rover!"
"Get down!"
"Bad dog!"

Rover eats dinner.

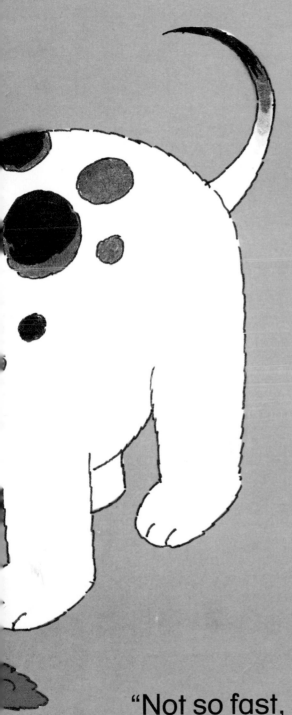

"Not so fast, Rover!
Slow down!"

Later, Amy and I get
ready for bed.

"I want Rover to sleep
on *my* bed," says Amy.

"I want Rover to sleep
on *my* bed," I say.

"Rover can sleep in his *own* bed,"
Mom and Dad say together.